To Evelyn – C.R.

First published in Great Britain in 1997 by
Frances Lincoln Limited, 4 Torriano Mews,
Torriano Avenue, London NW5 2RZ

First paperback edition 1999

British Library Cataloguing in Publication Data
available on request.

ISBN 0-7112-1129-9 paperback

Printed in China

7986

until I Met Dudley

How everyday things really work

ROGER M^{C}GOUGH
Illustrated by **CHRIS RIDDELL**

FRANCES LINCOLN

I thought I knew how a toaster worked...

When you put the slices of bread into the toaster and push the handle down, an alarm goes off underground, alerting the toast gnomes who spring into action. A friendly dragon toasts the bread with his fiery breath (although sometimes he breathes too hard!). Cog-wheels and conveyor belts, treadmills and telescopes - it's all so simple!

until I met Dudley...

Dudley showed me how a toaster works...

1. A toaster needs electricity to work... so... check it's plugged in and that the power is switched on. Pop a slice of bread (or 2 if you're hungry!) into the slots in the top. The bread nestles inside the toaster on a **rack** that is attached to a **spring**.

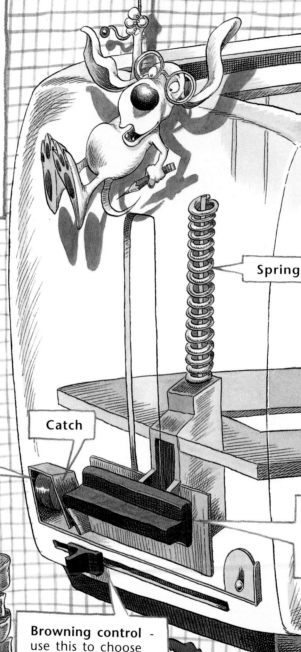

Spring

Bread rack

Catch

Electromagnet

Handle - gently push down the handle of your toaster and feel how springy it is.

2. *ZZZZPP!* When you pull the toaster handle down, the spring s-t-r-e-t-c-h-e-s and the rack moves down. *CLICK!* The rack is now locked in position with a small **catch**.

Browning control - use this to choose how dark you want your toast.

3. The electricity zooms along tiny wires woven together, called **heating elements**, either side of the bread. They are so hot that they start to glow, heating up the soft bread and turning it into toast.

4. When the elements heat up, so does a strip inside the toaster. As it is made of two different metals, it's called a **bimetallic strip**. When it gets hot, one of the metals expands more than the other. This makes it bend so it touches the **tripping plate**.

Heating elements - tiny wires woven in and out of thin non-metallic sheets.

Bimetallic strip

Tripping plate

POP!

Out comes tasty toast. Pass the marmalade, Dudley...

5. As soon as the bimetallic strip and tripping plate touch... *POW!*.. they make an electric circuit, or path.

6. Then the electricity surges along the path into an **electromagnet**. As the electric current passes through the magnet, it trips the catch that holds down the rack, then... *BOING!*.. The rack springs up and...

You load the dishwasher, put in the detergent, then switch on. The switch is linked to a special siren which emits a high-pitched whistle that can only be heard by cats.

At the signal, all the cats in the neighbourhood come running to your house and climb into the machine through the specially designed cat-flap at the back (that's the banging you hear). They lick all the plates, cups, pans and cutlery clean, singing happily to themselves (that's the humming you hear).

When everything is spick and span, they leave, last one out sprinkling the detergent around the machine to get rid of any catty smells.

until I met Dudley...

Dudley showed me how a dishwasher works...

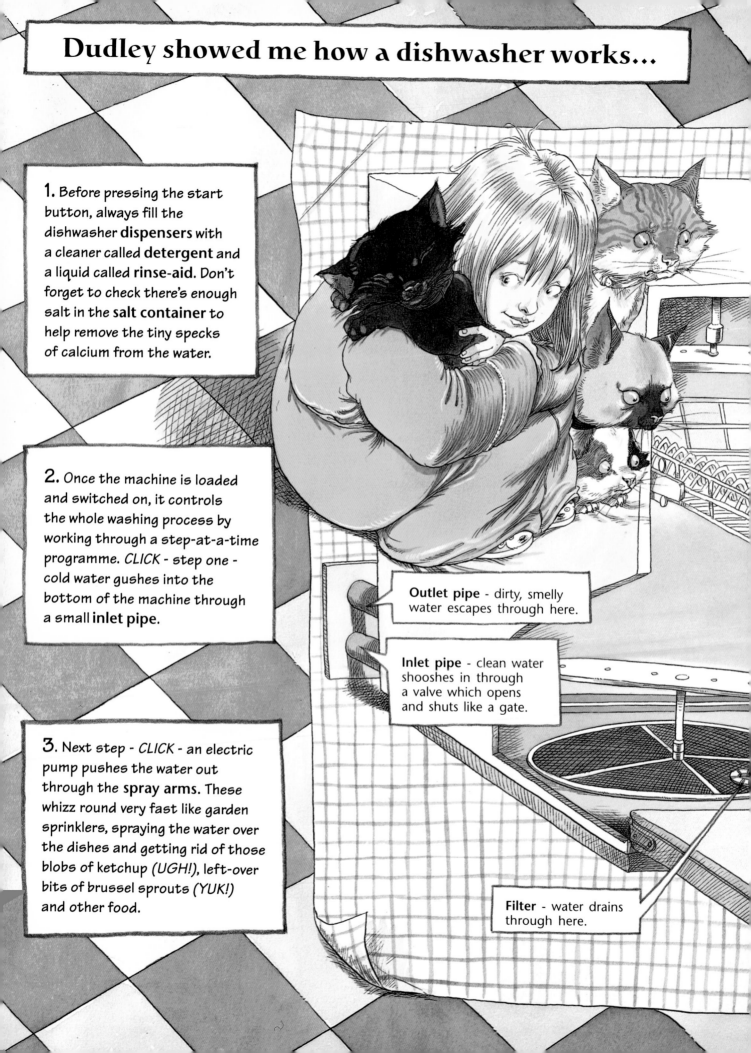

1. Before pressing the start button, always fill the dishwasher **dispensers** with a cleaner called **detergent** and a liquid called **rinse-aid**. Don't forget to check there's enough salt in the **salt container** to help remove the tiny specks of calcium from the water.

2. Once the machine is loaded and switched on, it controls the whole washing process by working through a step-at-a-time programme. *CLICK* - step one - cold water gushes into the bottom of the machine through a small **inlet pipe**.

3. Next step - *CLICK* - an electric pump pushes the water out through the **spray arms**. These whizz round very fast like garden sprinklers, spraying the water over the dishes and getting rid of those blobs of ketchup *(UGH!)*, left-over bits of brussel sprouts *(YUK!)* and other food.

Outlet pipe - dirty, smelly water escapes through here.

Inlet pipe - clean water shooshes in through a valve which opens and shuts like a gate.

Filter - water drains through here.

4. Then the dirty water drains down through a hole covered with a sieve-like **filter**. This works like a fishing net, catching all the bits of food that have been washed off the dishes. Remember to clean the filter from time to time, removing any food that is still there.

5. So what happens to all that dirty water? It disappears through another pipe called an **outlet pipe**... *GURGLE, GURGLE...* and eventually into the drain outside. *CLICK!* Clean water rushes into the bottom of the machine. This mixes with the detergent, heats up and sprays out of the whizzing arms to clean the dishes.

6. *WHOOSH!* Cold water pours in again and mixes with the rinse-aid liquid to rinse the detergent off the dishes. The mixture heats up, sprays out and then drains away through the outlet pipe, leaving the dishes to dry.

Spray arm- water sprays out through the tiny holes.

Washing-up basket

Salt container

Detergent dispenser

Rinse-aid dispenser

Programme dial - to choose and control the dishwashing steps.

I thought I knew how a fridge worked...

Special polar bears arrive every night to deliver blocks of ice cut from icebergs floating in the oceans of the Arctic. They pack the fridge with the ice and make sure everything is cold enough before leaving - which explains those paw-prints in the chocolate mousse.

As the ice begins to melt, water runs down the back of the fridge into a secret compartment at the bottom. Here, it flows into a water-wheel which drives a fan that spins cool air to keep the fridge cold.

until I met Dudley…

Dudley showed me how a fridge works...

1. The fridge is a big box which keeps food cold so that it stays fresh longer. It uses an ingredient called a refrigerant which runs round and round pipes hidden in the walls of the fridge.

2. On its journey around the maze of pipes, the refrigerant removes heat from the inside of the fridge, keeping it cool. It does this by changing from a runny liquid to an invisible gas.

3. The refrigerant begins its journey as a gas. It is then compressed by an electric pump called a **compressor**. The compressor squeezes the gas into a small space where at high pressure, it starts to turn into a liquid.

4. The gas changing to liquid gives off heat as it is pumped through a long snake-like tube called a **condenser**, on the outside of the fridge. Heat passes through the tube into the open air, like heat coming out of a radiator. That's why the back of a fridge feels hot.

5. Then, as the cold liquid flows into a wider tube in the **evaporator**, the pressure falls and... hey presto! The liquid turns back into a gas.

Evaporator - here the liquid turns to gas and absorbs heat.

Condenser - heat passes through here into the open air.

Compressor - this works like a heart, pumping the refrigerant round the fridge.

Foam or fibre glass insulation - this pads the walls of the fridge to stop cold air escaping or warm air sneaking in.

Thermostat - this can be altered to make the inside of the fridge colder or warmer. It controls how hard the compressor works. Number 1 is cool, number 5 is very, very chilly.

The Refrigerant's Journey.

③ Evaporator

Heat passes into the open air.

② Condenser

① Compressor

6. *BBRRRRR!* The cold gas starts to absorb all the heat from inside the fridge, like a bath sponge absorbing water. That's how the fridge is kept so cool inside.

7. The warm gas now continues its journey through a pipe, back to the compressor pump where it begins another cycle round the fridge.

Dust is the favourite food of the Hoover-Snake.
He sleeps curled up inside the tube until the
vacuum cleaner is switched on. He has a huge
appetite and is a noisy eater, gobbling up
all the dust, crumbs, buttons and Lego he can find.

When a Hoover-Snake is full, he waits until midnight, then slithers outside and sneezes! Trouble is, he always leaves the door wide open so that the wind blows the dust back in.

until I met Dudley...

Dudley showed me how a vacuum cleaner works...

1. A vacuum cleaner is powered by a mini **motor** that runs on electricity. So, before switching it on, it needs to be plugged into a nearby socket.

2. *WHIRRRR!* Once the motor is running, it turns a **fan** round and round. As the fan spins, it pushes air out of the vacuum cleaner through a tube called a **duct**.

3. Because air is pushed *out* of the cleaner, air gets sucked *in* to take its place, just like water being sucked up through a straw.

4. And as air gets sucked up through the **hose**, so does dirt and dust.

5. *SSLLUUUUP!* All this dust is then sucked into a **bag**. But where does the air go? It escapes through tiny holes in the walls of the bag. The dirt and dust are trapped inside - they're too big to get through the holes.

6. The bag fills up and after a while, needs emptying or replacing. If you don't keep an eye on it, it becomes so full that it...

Hose

Duct

Electric motor

Fan

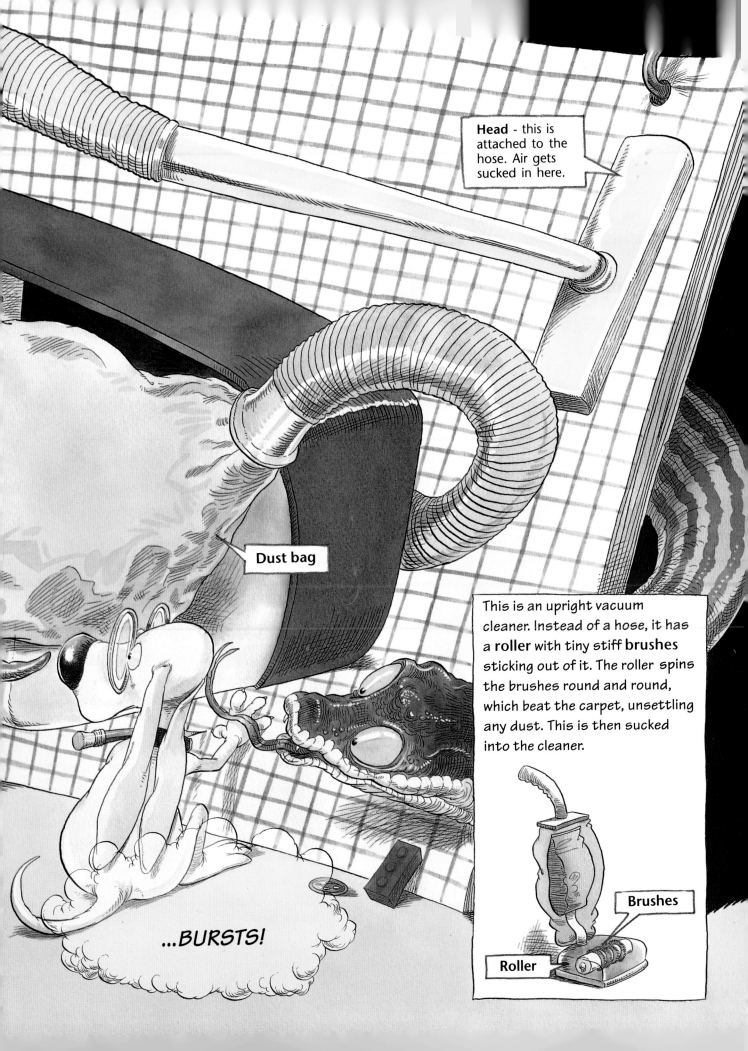

Head - this is attached to the hose. Air gets sucked in here.

Dust bag

...BURSTS!

This is an upright vacuum cleaner. Instead of a hose, it has a **roller** with tiny stiff **brushes** sticking out of it. The roller spins the brushes round and round, which beat the carpet, unsettling any dust. This is then sucked into the cleaner.

Brushes

Roller

until I met Dudley…

Dudley showed me how a rubbish truck works...

Warning light

1. A rubbish truck is a big bin on wheels, usually worked by a team of 3 or 4 people. The driver sits in the cab. He keeps the engine running to provide the power for the rubbish truck to do its job.

2. The other refuse collectors in the team pick up rubbish bins and heave them onto **the platform** at the back of the truck... *CLONK, CLINK, CLUNK.* **Clamps** hold the bins firmly so they can't fall off.

3. The platform, powered by the truck's engine, swings up... *WHIRRRR...* and tips the rubbish out of the bins, into the truck. Then the platform swings down so the refuse collectors can lift off the empty bins and put them back where they belong.

4. Inside the back of the truck there is a wide **scoop** which operates like a huge hand. It is attached to a powerful arm, called a **hydraulic ram**. The ram and scoop work together... *CRRUNCH... SQUUISH*, scooping and squashing the rubbish into the truck.

Warning light

Hydraulic ram - A ram has two parts: a long rod called a piston, fitted snugly inside a hollow tube called a cylinder. The piston slides backwards and forwards in the cylinder, just like the tube inside a bicycle pump.

Oil supply line - oil is pumped through here into the cylinder. The oil pushes the piston forwards and backwards which moves the ram.

Rubbish container

Ejector

Cylinder - the piston fits inside this hollow tube.

Piston - this slides backwards and forwards in the cylinder.

Hydraulic ram - which pushes the ejector forward or pulls it back

Clamps - these hold the bins.

Scoop

Platform

5. Once the truck is full of rubbish, it is driven to the depot where it is emptied. The driver presses another button... WHHIRRRR... and the back of the truck tips up. The **ejector**, a big metal wedge powered by another hydraulic ram, slides backwards... GRRMMMM... to push all the rubbish out of the truck.

Until I met Dudley I imagined all sorts of crazy things. I thought I knew...

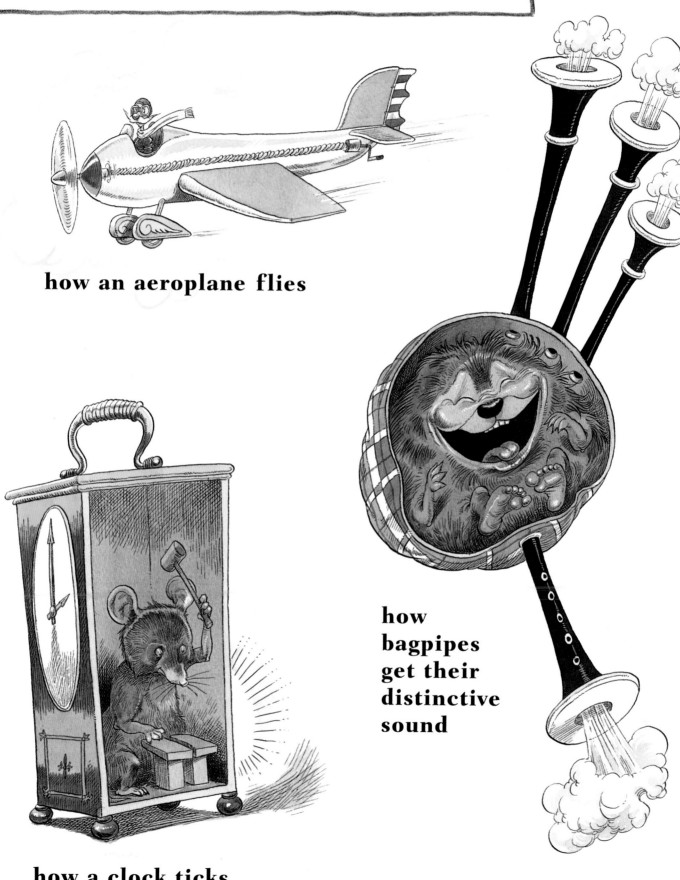

how an aeroplane flies

how bagpipes get their distinctive sound

how a clock ticks

how large ships keep afloat

how bubbles get into fizzy drinks

how stars
shine at night

I'm really glad I met him...

...I think!

MORE PICTURE BOOKS IN PAPERBACK
FROM FRANCES LINCOLN

HOW GREEN ARE YOU?
David Bellamy

Illustrated by Penny Dann

Can a six year-old help to save the world? Renowned conservationist David Bellamy says yes! In this fun and informative book, the Friendly Whale leads us on a tour of our every-day habitat, explaining how we can protect the environment at every step.

Suitable for National Curriculum Science – Key Stages 1 and 2; Geography, Key Stages 1 and 2
Scottish Guidelines Environmental Studies, Levels B and C

ISBN 0-7112-0679-1

THE PEBBLE IN MY POCKET
Meredith Hooper

Illustrated by Chris Coady

Where do pebbles come from? How were they made? Remarkable text and stunning pictures evoke the drama of the Earth's history as we follow the processes of rock-formation and erosion that create pebbles all over the world.

Shortlisted for the British Society for the History of Science Dingle Book Prize 1997

Suitable for National Curriculum English – Reading, Key Stages 2 and 3; Science, Key Stages 2 and 3
Scottish Guidelines English Language – Reading, Level D; Environmental Studies, Level D

ISBN 0-7112-1076-4

OUTSIDE-IN
Clare Smallman

Illustrated by Edwina Riddell

An entertaining and informative tour of the body, with lift-up flaps to explain what really happens when we look from the outside in.

Suitable for National Curriculum Science, Key Stages 1 and 2; English – Reading, Key Stages 1 and 2
Scottish Guidelines Environmental Studies – Health, Levels A, B and C; English Language – Reading, Level B

ISBN 0-7112-0774-7

Frances Lincoln titles are available from all good bookshops